Starring Grace

MARY HOFFMAN

PICTURES BY CAROLINE BINCH

PUFFIN BOOKS

For Caroline,
who makes stories come true
M.H.

PUFFIN BOOKS
Published by the Penguin Group
Penguin Putnam Books for Young Readers,
345 Hudson Street, New York, New York 10014, U.S.A.
Penguin Books Ltd, 27 Wrights Lane, London W8 5TZ, England
Penguin Books Australia Ltd, Ringwood, Victoria, Australia
Penguin Books Canada Ltd, 10 Alcorn Avenue, Toronto, Ontario, Canada M4V 3B2
Penguin Books (N.Z.) Ltd, 182-190 Wairau Road, Auckland 10, New Zealand

Penguin Books Ltd, Registered Offices: Harmondsworth, Middlesex, England

First published in the United States of America by Phyllis Fogelman Books,
an imprint of Penguin Putnam Books for Young Readers, 2000
Published by Puffin Books,
a division of Penguin Putnam Books for Young Readers, 2001

1 3 5 7 9 10 8 6 4 2

Library of Congress Cataloging-in-Publication Data information available upon request.

Puffin Books ISBN 0-14-230022-5

Printed in the United States of America

RL: 3.0

Contents

⁕⁕⁕⁕

Grace and the Big Top

It was the beginning of summer vacation, and the weeks stretched out ahead of Grace like a new country to explore. Her family wasn't going away, but later Ma was getting some time off and Nana was going to visit a friend.

Grace didn't mind. Some of her friends were going to camp, but four were going to be around all summer: her best friend, Aimee, plus Kester and Raj and Maria.

"Ma," asked Grace as soon as school was out, "can we have our headquarters here in our apartment?"

"Who's 'we'?" asked Ma.

"Me and Aimee and the others. We are the only ones not going anywhere, and I'm the only one with no brothers and sisters to get in the way. Besides, we've got a backyard. So can we play here every day? They could bring a bag lunch, just like at school."

"That's okay with me, as long as you don't eat me right out of cookies," said Ma. "But you must check with Nana. She's the one who will be home all day with you."

Nana was happy about it. "I like having lots of kids around. You know that, Grace."

It was true. All the children in the neighborhood treated Grace's nana as if she were their own grandmother, and that was mainly because she treated them as if they were her grandchildren.

So every day Grace's four friends gathered at her apartment and thought of things they could be. In the first week they were pirates, then mountaineers, then knights, then aliens. By Friday they had run out of new things to play.

"We should be a gang and give ourselves a name," said Kester.

"What?" said Aimee. "Like the Famous Five?"

"But we're not famous," objected Grace. "We'd have to be the Five No One Has Heard Of."

"That doesn't sound very exciting," said Raj.

"How about the Red Hand Gang?"

"But we don't do crimes," said Maria.

"What *do* we do?" asked Aimee. "We just hang out and have fun."

"We have adventures," said Grace. "That's what we do. And we need a new one."

Just then Nana came out and showed them a brightly colored advertisement that had been put in the mailbox. It said:

THE CIRCUS IS COMING!
SIGNOR SPARKY'S ONE-DAY
SPECTACLE!

See the Flying Fandango Sisters, Horatio the Fire-Eater, Manuel the Magnificent, the Strongest Man in the World, Lady Magnolia and her Famous Troupe of Dancing Horses, the Breath-Taking Balancing Act of Boris the Brave Tightrope Walker, the Incredible Antics of the Gravity-Defying Garibaldi Family of Acrobats, and our Own Beloved Clowns, Bongo and Bertie. All hosted by your Ringmaster, the Supreme, the Incomparable SIGNOR SPARKY!

Well, after that, there was no question about what the children would be playing for the rest of the day. Grace got Nana to promise she would take her to the circus on Saturday. Then the gang set to work in the backyard.

First they made a big circle with string and pegs. Then Grace rummaged in her dress-up box. She found lots of flowery dresses and bright scarves that had been Nana's, and best of all, a collapsible black hat.

"That's what you call an opera hat," said Nana, shaking the flat black circle so that it turned into a top hat. "It belonged to your grandpa."

"Can we have it for a ringmaster's hat?" asked Grace.

"Why not?" said Nana. "There's a cane too. Your grandpa used to tap-dance."

"It should be a whip, really," said Grace. "But we don't have any animals, and besides, a whip is cruel, so a cane is better. It could be a magic wand too."

So now they had a ring and a ringmaster's outfit. Nana put her foot down about tightrope-walking along the clothesline, trapeze acts hanging from the tree-swing, or any form of fire-eating. But that still left plenty of acts.

Being acrobats was the most popular one.

Everybody wanted to be a Garibaldi, and there was a lot of rolling around, doing somersaults, and leapfrogging.

When they were tired of that, Kester said he was going to be Manuel the Magnificent and show off his strength. First he picked up a deck chair with one hand—almost. Then he got the others to tie him up in a jump rope and he burst out of it. Actually, he sort of untied it, but it looked good.

"I know," said Grace. She got out her face paints and gave Kester a curly black mustache. "Now you really look the part."

"I want to be Lady Magnolia," said Maria, "but we'll have to make up the horses."

Grace dressed Maria in bright scarves and gave her an old hobbyhorse to ride. Raj and Aimee wanted to be Bongo and Bertie the clowns. Some more face paint soon gave them red noses and big smiles.

"You'll have to be Signor Sparky, Grace," said Aimee.

Grace didn't at all mind wearing Grandpa's top hat and waving the cane. After a lot of practicing, it was time for Ma to come home from work. Grace was ready for her.

"Step right up!" she shouted as soon as Ma was inside the door. "Come to the circus! Nana too," she added in her ordinary voice.

So Ma and Nana sat in deck chairs drinking iced tea, while Grace introduced all the acts. Kester escaped from the jump rope, Maria galloped around the ring on her hobbyhorse and even jumped through Grace's old hula hoop. Raj and Maria sprayed each other with silly string and made a big mess with buckets of water. Then everyone changed back into shorts and T-shirts and became Garibaldis, but they got very wet because of all the water the clowns had spilled on the grass.

At the end Grace quickly put her top hat back on so she could introduce all the circus performers to take their bows.

"Bravo! Hooray!" shouted Ma and Nana, clapping as hard as they could.

After a snack the circus acts all went home, but Grace kept the top hat on at dinner and even wore it in the bathtub.

"Nana says we can go to the circus tomorrow. We can, can't we, Ma?" she asked at bedtime.

"I daresay we can," said Ma. "But I doubt it will be as good as your circus."

"But there will be real horses, and all the things Nana wouldn't let us do, like fire-eating."

"Nana was quite right about that," said Ma.

The next day Grace could hardly contain her excitement. She fidgeted all morning and ate her lunch so fast that she couldn't remember what it was.

In the afternoon they went to the local park, where a big striped tent was now standing. They took Aimee with them, and Grace insisted on wearing the top hat. All the children in the neighborhood seemed to have read Signor Sparky's advertisement and persuaded their parents to bring them to the circus. Kester and Raj and Maria were in the ticket line and they got seats close together.

There was a real band playing circus music. Then there was a big drum roll and Signor Sparky strode into the center of the ring. He had a red suit and a black top hat, a long black whip and a megaphone, through which he shouted "Step right up!" in the most satisfactory way.

The next hour and a half was total magic. The children laughed at the clowns, gasped at the tightrope walker, and loved the Garibaldis. Lady Magnolia wore a sparkly pink leotard and had huge pink plumes in her hair and on her bottom, and she rode two gray horses at the same time. Manuel the Magnificent ended his act by lifting Lady Magnolia right off the ground. And he *did* have a curly black mustache, which looked perfectly real.

After the intermission Signor Sparky asked for a volunteer from the audience, and all the children in the tent waved their arms in the air. His eye lighted on Grace. He picked up his megaphone and said in a loud voice, "I'll have the little girl with the top hat. I could do with an assistant ringmaster."

So Grace got to join the circus. She was given the megaphone and told to announce Horatio the Fire-Eater. She was so close to him, she could feel the heat of the flaming torches. Then there was a knife-throwing act, jugglers, and more from the clowns. Bongo squirted water from a flower in his buttonhole right into Grace's eye!

"And finally," shouted Signor Sparky, "before I introduce our last act, let's give a big hand to our little ringmaster, Signorina Gracia!"

There was a lot of clapping as Grace went back to her seat.

"Lucky!" whispered Aimee.

The next act was the Flying Fandango Sisters on the trapeze, and then the circus was over.

"Did you have a good day?" asked Ma as she tucked Grace into bed that night.

"The best!" said Grace. "I've been in the real circus."

"Yes," said Ma. "That's two circuses in two days. But I think you'll sleep more comfortably if you take that hat off!"

Grace and the Haunted House

The week after the circus felt a bit flat. After a few halfhearted attempts to learn juggling—which was much harder than it looked in the big top—the children tired of their circus acts and were ready for a new adventure.

"We could be ghostbusters," Kester suggested.

"But there are no ghosts to bust," objected Maria.

"There's no such thing as ghosts anyway," Raj said scornfully.

"What about the haunted house, Grace?" asked Aimee.

Everybody sat up and looked expectantly at Grace. "Well," she began slowly, "we don't know that it *is* haunted for sure."

"We always used to call it that, though," said Aimee.

It was true. The year before, Grace and Aimee had gotten a little obsessed with the house whose backyard faced Grace's. For weeks they had played a game that the house was haunted, but Ma had gotten mad and told them not to be silly. Like Raj, Ma didn't believe in ghosts and she thought it was a bad game to play.

That's why Grace was hesitant about telling the others about it now. But they needed a new game and the haunted house was temptingly close by. Besides, everyone had comics with ghosts in them, and they all read books and saw movies that were spooky. In fact, it was the most popular sort of entertainment among their schoolmates.

"Go on, Grace," said Kester. "Tell us about the house."

"It's *that* one," said Grace, settling into her storytelling position with her back against the tree, and pointing to the house beyond the fence. Four pairs of eyes obediently swiveled around to look.

"Ever since we've lived here," Grace went on, "which is as long as I can remember, we've never seen anyone in that backyard. It's all overgrown, with long weeds and nettles, and the house has bars on all the windows."

"Perhaps it's empty," said Raj.

"No," said Grace. "The mailman and the paperboy both deliver there, and once a week groceries come in a van."

"Maybe it's a hideout for thieves," suggested Maria.

"Or a safe house for witness protection," said Kester.

"Could be," said Grace, "but that doesn't explain the howling in the night."

This produced the desired effect, since her four friends asked with one voice, "What howling in the night?"

"You remember, Aimee," said Grace. "I told you about it last year. It doesn't happen every night. But sometimes it wakes me up. An eerie, ghosty sort of noise that floats through the darkness."

"What does it sound like?" asked Maria.

"Like a soul in torment," said Grace, and gave them a bloodcurdling demonstration.

"I vote we go over the fence and explore," said Raj, jumping to his feet.

Now there was going to be trouble, thought Grace. She knew that Nana wouldn't approve of their going into the neighboring backyard, but she also knew that Nana was taking a little nap. And besides, all the others had voted in favor. She couldn't hold out against them, particularly when she was the one who had told them about the house.

So over the fence they went. The backyard was overgrown with waist-high grass that had not been cut for years. Where the flower beds used to be, there was nothing but nettles, and there were brambles hidden in the long grass. The ghost-hunters got a lot of scratches on their legs and arms as they cautiously approached the house.

It wasn't full of towers and pointed roofs like a haunted house in the movies. It was a small square house, with small square windows.

"See," hissed Aimee. "There are the bars."

It was true. Every window had a metal grating like the kind you see on the windows of jewelers' shops.

"Maybe an eccentric millionaire lives there," whispered Maria.

"Yeah," agreed Kester. "There's probably loads of jewels and gold stuff lying around, and the millionaire is scared of burglars."

"What do you think, Grace?" asked Aimee.

"I think we should go back," said Grace. She was trying to remember something Nana had told her about the house.

"Don't be lame," said Kester. "We just got here."

Just then an eerie shriek pierced the still air of the overgrown backyard. The children stood frozen with terror, then raced for the fence, tearing their clothes on thorns as they ran. They tumbled back into Grace's yard, trembling.

"*Now* do you believe me?" asked Grace, although she herself hadn't really believed that the house was haunted until she heard the howling in broad daylight.

"It's haunted, all right," said Aimee, her eyes as big as saucers.

"There must be some explanation," said Raj.

"But what?" asked Kester.

"And what do we do about it?" asked Maria.

But nobody had any ideas then.

Nana was very suspicious when she called them in to wash their hands before lunch. "What on earth do you find to do in our pocket handkerchief of a backyard to get you all so filthy? And how did you get those scratches?"

Grace made up a story about teasing Paw-Paw the cat, and the children kept their worst wounds out of sight while Grace fetched the antiseptic cream.

The children ate their sandwiches and potato chips while they discussed a plan.

"We need real ghost-hunting equipment," said Kester. "We could make some out of odds and ends."

"Yes, but it wouldn't have real electricity or plasma in it," said Raj, "so it wouldn't really work. It would only be pretend."

"But you think ghosts are pretend, anyway," said Maria, and Raj had no answer to that.

So they went to Grace's recycling bins and found cardboard tubes and boxes that looked good when stuck together and colored with markers. But there was only enough for one ghost-hunting pack. They drew straws to see who should carry it, and Kester won. The others would have to be decoys and reporters.

"One of us should go around to the front and ring the doorbell," said Maria.

"I'll do it," said Raj. "And I'll keep whoever opens the door chatting, while you try and get in the back."

"No one will open the door," said Grace. "Whoever lives in that house really doesn't like people."

"Well, it's our best chance," said Maria. "Let's try."

The ghost-hunters climbed over the fence again and through the long grass. There was one scary moment when they heard the grass rustling behind them, but it turned out to be Paw-Paw stalking them as part of a game of his own.

The back of the house was just as still and blank as before. All the window frames were painted brown, and you couldn't see through the metal gratings because the beige curtains inside were tightly drawn. Raj slipped around to the front of the house and the others tried the back door. Grace felt really bad about it—she thought it was too much like burgling. But the door was firmly locked anyway.

"It'll be no good if someone *does* answer the front door," groaned Kester. "We can't get in the back."

They all heard the doorbell ring at the same time. Raj rang three times, very loudly. The others heard a movement inside the house. The doorbell rang again. Then someone crept up behind the children. They jumped several feet in the air. It was Raj.

"What are you doing here?" cried Aimee. "You nearly gave us a heart attack."

Raj was panting. "I rang the bell, but no one came. Then this van drove up and a man came out and walked to the front door. He gave me a suspicious look, so I bolted."

"He's probably a conspirator," said Maria excitedly.

"No, wait," said Grace. "It's Monday afternoon, isn't it? That's when the grocery van comes."

Just then a voice came calling over the backyards. "*Gra-a-ace!* GRACE! Where are you?"

"Oh no," groaned Grace. "It's Nana. She'll

know we've been in this backyard. We are going to be in so much trouble."

"And just why are you in my backyard?" said a voice from the haunted house. One of the curtains was drawn back, a window had been opened, and an ancient face covered in wrinkles was peering out through the bars.

"Stay where you are," said the face, and the children heard the unlocking of the back door. There was enough clanking of chains to satisfy the keenest ghost-hunter. The children stood stock-still, caught between the wrath of Nana and whatever was going to come out of the back door of the haunted house.

It was a tiny old lady, the sort you see in fairy tale illustrations. She walked very slowly with a stick, and her hands were gnarled and twisted— like a witch, thought Grace—but her face was kind and her dark eyes were bright in her wrinkled face. She turned to Raj. "Why were you ringing my doorbell, young man? I saw you from the front window, while I was waiting for my groceries." Her voice was deep and she had a foreign accent.

Raj didn't know what to say. The old woman

looked at Kester and his bundle of tubes and boxes. "What's that contraption?" she asked.

"It's for catching ghosts," said Kester, who was a truthful boy.

There was a funny, rusty, grating noise, and the children realized that the old woman was trying to laugh.

"Did you think I was a ghost, then?" she asked.

"Not exactly," said Grace, "but we heard these ghostly noises coming from your house. We're really very sorry. We didn't mean to disturb you."

Just then Paw-Paw came stalking out from the grass and rubbed himself around the old woman's legs. Grace held her breath.

"Oh, what a beautiful pusskin," said the old woman and bent to stroke him.

"He's our cat," said Grace. "We call him Paw-Paw."

"Good name for a cat," said the old woman. "I call mine Jauler, which is German for 'Howler.' I wonder if you can guess why."

A long, pointed, handsome face peeped around the door, at the level of the woman's ankles. It was chocolate-colored with blue eyes. A thin cream-colored body with very long legs followed. When the new cat saw Paw-Paw, he arched his back and hissed. Then he let out a long, unearthly howl. At first the children froze, then they relaxed and began to smile.

"Here is your ghost, no?" said the old woman.

Grace breathed a sigh of relief. Not only was the house not haunted, but the old woman didn't seem angry with them for trespassing in her backyard. Then Grace remembered Nana.

"We'd better go," she said politely. "And we really are sorry that we thought your house was haunted. It was only a game."

"Ah," said the old woman sadly. "I didn't say it wasn't haunted. Only that my cat is no ghost. But, listen, your grandmother is calling you. You can tell her I asked you to help find my cat. She knows I don't like him to go out."

Grace gasped. "You know my nana?"

"A little," said the old woman. "I don't have many friends."

"We'll be your friends, if you like," said Aimee.

The old woman looked at her and a series of

strange expressions flitted across her face.

"I should like that," she said. "Come back to-morrow and I'll have some pastries ready for you." Then she picked up her Siamese cat, who draped himself over her shoulders like a scarf, and went back indoors. The children heard the bolts and chains.

"Pastries!" said Kester as they ran back through the long grass. "That's just like the witch in the gingerbread house. She probably wants to eat us."

"Don't be so silly," said Maria. "She was a nice old lady."

"Nana won't let us go back unless she knows it's safe," said Grace. "She doesn't let me talk to strangers."

Nana needed a lot of calming down once the children had scrambled back over the fence. After a while she listened to what they were telling her.

"That's Gerda Myerson," she said eventually. "I'm amazed she asked you to help her. Gerda keeps herself to herself."

"But why?" asked Grace, who didn't feel that the whole mystery of the house had been explained. After all, the old woman had agreed it was haunted. "And why does she have all those locks and bars?"

Nana hesitated. "Gerda Myerson had some bad experiences during the war," she said at last. "Very bad. Her whole family was killed, and she was imprisoned for a long time. She survived and came to live in this country. But she finds it hard to trust people and she keeps her house all locked up, to make herself feel safe."

"Can we go and see her again tomorrow?" asked Grace. "She invited us and said she'd give us pastries."

Nana laughed. "Well, I see she knows the best way to get you to be her friends. Yes, you can go. It's a good sign that Gerda asked you. Perhaps she finds children less frightening than grown-ups. But promise me you will never, ever go out of this backyard again without telling me where you are going. You scared me out of my wits."

All the ghost-hunters promised.

Grace Goes on Safari

The next day the gang was all for going straight back into the overgrown backyard.

"Not yet," said Aimee. "She won't have had time to make the pastries."

"You don't know that she's going to make them," said Raj. "She might have had some delivered by the grocer."

"Why would an old lady living on her own order enough pastries to feed five children?" asked Kester.

"I would, if I was an old lady," said Maria.

Grace said, "Let's think of what we're going to do when we get there. I have an idea."

Everyone looked at Grace.

"It's the perfect kind of backyard to be a jungle," she said.

Everyone started to talk at once. They hadn't played explorers yet this summer and Grace was right: The haunted house's backyard was the perfect place.

"We'll need supplies," said Grace. "And sun hats. And some things to be wild animals."

As usual Nana was roped in to help with what they needed for their game.

"You'll need lots of bottles of water if you're going on safari," she said. "The jungle is a thirsty place."

They found all sorts of old hats to wear as sun helmets. Nana let Grace have hers, the one she had worn when they went to The Gambia. It really did look a bit like a safari hat. And the star of the animal collection, which was made up mainly of soft bears and rabbits, was a huge wooden crocodile with white teeth, a souvenir they had brought back from West Africa.

"We should have a tent," said Raj. "Do you have one, Grace?"

Grace didn't, so they took some old sheets and a clothes-drying rack.

"We'll have to cut some grass before we can pitch a tent," said Maria. "We need a machete."

Nana didn't have a machete, but she gave them a blunt pair of backyard shears, with a lot of warnings to be careful.

It was a good thing that Mrs. Myerson knew they were coming. When she looked out of her back window, she saw five hats advancing through the grass and strange objects held high, including a large crocodile.

The children knocked on the back door.

"Good morning," said Grace when the old woman opened the door. "I hope we're not too early. We wondered if we could play safari in your backyard."

"I see you're all dressed for the part," said Mrs. Myerson. "You play as much as you like, and when you've had enough, knock again and I'll have a treat ready for you."

It was a glorious morning. The sun shone and it was very hot, just like in the real jungle. The children pretended that the flies were mosquitoes. They pulled leaves off one of the bigger weeds and used them to wave in front of their faces. Paw-Paw joined them and became a real tiger in the long grass.

They found a very small stagnant pond in one

corner of the yard, which Grace said was the great gray-green greasy Limpopo River. It was full of frogs and looked very realistic when they put Grace's crocodile on the bank.

Mrs. Myerson's backyard was no bigger than Grace's, but it seemed huge because it was so wild and overgrown. They pretended all the brambles in the grass were snakes, and they had to avoid being bitten.

When they got tired, they took turns using the shears to cut a patch of grass near the house and set up their drying-rack tent in the clearing they had made. There was room for two in it if they squeezed in very tightly. The others threw themselves down on the grass.

"I'm starving," said Kester. "Let's see about those pastries."

Gerda Myerson hobbled out with a tray of delicious-smelling pastries, which were a funny shape, twisted like pretzels, but covered with white icing sugar. They were full of raisins and almonds and the taste of cinnamon.

She sat on an old kitchen chair outside her back door and watched the children eat like hungry explorers.

"It is nice to sit in the sun again," she said in her deep rusty voice, "and I see you have been cutting my grass."

"I hope you don't mind," said Grace. "We needed somewhere for the tent."

But immediately Grace felt sorry that they had only cut the grass to fit their game.

As soon as Mrs. Myerson had gone indoors, an idea began to form in her mind for another game just as good.

"The Secret Garden," she said. "That's what this is. We could make it all nice for her again and then she could sit out in it."

"That's a girl's story," said Raj. "And if we cut all the grass, we won't be able to play safari anymore."

"But we've *played* that already," said Grace, who was always looking for new games. "Besides, there are boys in the Secret Garden. There's Dickon, who is fantastic with animals, and Colin, who is—"

"Pathetic," said Kester. "I'm not being him."

"But he stops being pathetic when he meets Mary," said Maria. "I should be her because I've got the right sort of name."

"I don't mean we should act out the Secret Garden," said Grace. "There's only three children in it and five of us. I mean we could make up a secret garden type of story of our own, while we clear this one up for Mrs. Myerson. After all, she did make us nice pastries—and she didn't tell on us to Nana yesterday."

In the end they all agreed. But they had to go back to Grace's and explain their plan to Nana. She thought it was a good idea and gave them some gardening gloves and trowels, and some black bags for the weeds and boxes for the brambles.

As soon as they had had their lunch, the safari team went back into the wild backyard.

"We're still explorers," said Grace. "Only we've stumbled on a secret backyard in the heart of the jungle. We need to make a big clearing, so that—"

"So that we can reach the holy temple in the middle of the backyard," said Aimee.

"Yes," said Kester. "And in the temple there's an old statue with a precious ruby in it."

"Worth millions of dollars," said Raj. "And if we find it, we can keep it."

It was only a small backyard and there were five of them, so it shouldn't have taken long to tidy up. But Nana hadn't given them any very sharp tools and there had been no weeding done for years. Cutting the grass was very hard too, since it was damp. When they had cleared a patch, it looked stubbly and yellow instead of smooth and green.

"Hey, I've found a wild orchid!" called Maria, who was weeding a flower bed.

They all came to see the bright red flower she had cleared from under the weeds. It was some sort of lily, but it looked exotic enough to be an orchid in the weedy flower bed.

"That'll cheer the old lady up," said Kester.

They speeded up after finding the flower, and by the end of the afternoon the side passage was full of bags and boxes of grass-cuttings and weeds. The old jungle had completely disappeared and the late-afternoon sun shone on a square of yellow lawn, three dug-over flower beds, and a small pond with reeds and frogs.

The children had found many stones and pebbles when they were digging and they piled the best ones up around the pond to look like a rock garden. The lumpy ones were put in the boxes with the brambles.

When they had finished, they saw Nana's face smiling over the fence.

"My, you've done a good job!" she said, looking at the secret garden. "Won't Gerda be pleased!"

At that moment, Mrs. Myerson came out of her back door. At first she didn't seem pleased at all. She looked at the backyard. Her face twisted and there were tears on her cheeks. Then she brushed them away with the back of her hand and smiled.

"Thank you," she said. "Thank you, my little explorers. You have discovered a lovely backyard for me. It reminds me of when I was a child, and the world was a sunnier place."

Then she walked across the still-damp grass to speak to Nana.

The explorers ate a huge snack at Grace's before going home. Their arms and legs ached and they were covered in fresh bramble scratches and nettle stings. But they were all happy.

"It's a pity about the jungle," said Raj.

"And we didn't find a precious jewel," said Kester.

"No," said Maria, "but my orchid was as red as a ruby."

"And the new backyard might be as precious as jewels to Mrs. Myerson," said Grace.

"I think you all did a very important thing today," said Nana. "Most of your games are just for fun and that's how it should be. But today you played a game that helped a frightened person come out and walk in the sunshine of her own backyard."

Grace had been feeling bad for a whole day about lying to Nana. Now she just had to own up.

"Yesterday we thought Mrs. Myerson was a ghost," she said. "We went into her backyard to find out. She didn't really ask us to help her catch her cat."

Nana looked serious for a moment. "She is a bit like a ghost. Or she used to be. You kids seem to be bringing her back to life."

"I thought she was a witch when we first saw her," admitted Aimee.

"Well, honey," said Nana, "there's more to

people than what they look like."

"Yeah," said Kester. "She makes great pastries."

They all laughed.

"That's two things you explorers discovered today, then," said Nana.

Grace Blasts Off

—◦◦◦—

Grace was having a hard time. Nana wasn't there. She had gone on vacation all by herself— a thing Grace couldn't remember ever happening before in her life.

"Of course you must go," Ma had said when Nana got the invitation from her old friend Coralita in Texas. "It will be the vacation of a lifetime."

So Nana had gone—for two whole weeks— and Grace wished she had gone with her. It wasn't that she and Ma didn't love each other, because they did, very much. But they weren't used to being on their own together. As long as Grace could remember, Nana had always been there, ready to hear about what had happened at school, or happy to tell Grace one of her stories, or just singing in the kitchen while she made dinner.

Now Grace was being looked after during the day by Aimee's mom, and the gang had to play at Aimee's house. Aimee's mom brought Grace back each evening when Ma returned from the hospital, where she worked as an administrator.

And when Ma did get in, Grace was usually bursting to tell what had happened during her day, how Aimee had new sneakers just like the kind Grace wanted, or what games the gang had played. But Ma was always so tired when she got home. She sat on the sofa and kicked off her leather shoes and said, "Make me a cup of tea, will you, honey?" and, "Could you fetch my slippers, please, sweetie? I've had such a bad day."

Of course, Grace didn't mind doing these things, but she wanted Ma to listen to stuff about her day too. Ma *would* listen, sort of. But she kept yawning and, after she drank her tea, she would often nod off for a while. Grace just had to be patient and watch TV and wait for her to wake up.

And Ma didn't seem to know any stories like Nana's, except what had happened at the hospital—how there were never enough beds for the sick people who needed them, and how she was always running around trying to find somewhere to put everyone.

When she woke up again, Ma made dinner, and she didn't sing while she did it. Grace helped her and that was their best time together. Grace made cold drinks for them both and set the table, and she and Ma did chat then. But, although Grace felt mean even thinking it, Ma didn't make such good food as Nana did.

Grace missed Nana's fried chicken and black-eyed beans. On the way home from work, Ma would just pick up something ready-made from the supermarket, something that could be cooked quickly in the oven or microwave. Grace didn't complain, because she knew how hard Ma worked and how tired she got. But she was a little bored with frozen french fries and microwave pizza.

Nana had been gone for over a week when Aimee's mom brought Grace home and Grace found an envelope with a beautiful stamp on it on the mat. The envelope had blue flowers and a Texas postmark.

Nana! thought Grace. But the letter was addressed to Ma.

As soon as Ma opened the door, Grace met her with a cup of tea and her slippers.

"Sit down, sit down, Ma," she said excitedly. "Here's your tea. And here's a letter from Nana! Open it and read it to me, please!"

"All right, all right," said Ma. "Let me get my breath." But she did open the letter. "Look, here's one inside just for you," she said. "And a photo. Oh, my! What *has* Nana done?"

Grace took the photo. And there was Nana's lovely familiar face, but she was dressed as an astronaut! Grace's eyes got bigger and bigger. "Nana hasn't gone up in space, has she?" she asked.

Ma laughed until the tears ran down her cheeks.

"Oh, honey, you should see your face! I don't think so, but let's read our letters and find out."

Grace's letter was hard to read. She wasn't used to reading Nana's handwriting. But what it said was very exciting. Nana had been to the NASA Space Center and seen Mission Control and eaten special space ice cream. And then she

had had her photo taken in a studio that made her look like an astronaut.

"Well, doesn't that beat everything!" said Ma. "My mother, the astronaut. I know that some older people are going up in space now, but I never thought I'd see your nana dressed up in a space suit and helmet."

Grace's eyes were shining. She had never thought of being an astronaut, but now her imagination was working overtime.

"Do you know any stories about space, Ma?" she asked.

"Well, I can tell you about the night I stayed up to watch the first people walk on the moon," said Ma. "In fact, why don't we go out and get Chinese food tonight and I'll tell you over dinner? I'm getting sick of my own cooking."

It was the best night since Nana had left. They had chow mein and fried rice and spring rolls and pancakes with a spicy sauce, and Grace ate as much as she possibly could. So did Ma, and she told Grace about when she was a little girl, much younger than Grace was now, and they had seen the first people on the moon.

"We didn't have our own TV then—imagine!—so we went to a neighbor's house. In fact, it was Coralita's house, you know, the friend Nana is staying with now. There were about a dozen kids crammed on the sofa, all very sleepy because it was way past our bedtime, and then the landing was delayed, so it got even later. I kept dozing off and then your nana shook me awake and said, 'Look, look, Ava, that's the moon and that man coming down the ladder will be the first person ever to step on it.' I couldn't believe it. I mean, it was all just like a dusty old desert, not a bit like the shiny, silvery moon Nana used to take me out to see on clear nights."

Maybe Ma didn't tell the story as well as Nana would have done, but it was a story all the same and Grace was fascinated by it. Over the weekend she borrowed all the space books she could find in the library and played astronauts with the gang. She showed them the photo and told them that Nana was going into space.

"I'm Mae Jemison," said Grace, "and I'm launching my shuttle. Ten . . . nine . . . eight . . . seven . . . six . . . five . . . four . . . three . . . two . . . one—BLAST OFF!"

And she ran around the backyard with her arms out wide, flapping them so hard, she nearly did take off. Aimee and Raj and Kester and Maria were at Grace's house, and there was only one game they wanted to play. They pretended there was no gravity by walking slowly around the yard, taking huge steps and bouncing slowly up and down.

"I'm going to be an astronaut when I grow up," said Grace.

"So am I," said Kester. "It's the best job. You get to be weightless and eat dried food, so you don't have to wash the dishes."

"Me too," said the others.

"But we can't be astronauts without a space-ship," said Grace. "Let's build one!"

So they found a lot of cardboard boxes and some crates that Nana's marmalade oranges had come in, and tied them together with string. It didn't look very much like a spaceship when they had finished, but two small astronauts could just about squeeze into the "capsule" at the same time. They took turns.

But blasting off was difficult; the spaceship always toppled over.

"I know," said Grace. "Let's prop it up against the tree so it's upright."

It was Grace's turn to be captain. Aimee was her navigator and the others were Mission Control. It was much more difficult to get into the spaceship now that it was propped against the tree.

"Okay," said Raj. "All systems are go. Prepare for liftoff. Ten . . . nine . . . eight . . ."

By the time he got to three, the spaceship was wobbling alarmingly. Aimee was trying to make herself more comfortable in the crate and Grace was trying to keep it steady. When Raj reached BLAST OFF! the whole contraption collapsed and Grace and Aimee fell out in a heap.

"Ow!" yelled Aimee. "You're sitting on my hand! It really hurts."

Grace had a bump on her head that was growing before their eyes. But Aimee was clutching her wrist with her other hand and her face had gotten very white. Hearing the noise, Ma came running out into the yard. She took one look at the astronauts and sent Mission Control home. Then she called Aimee's mom and they took the two girls to the doctor.

Grace was given a big bandage on her forehead and Aimee had her arm put in a sling.

"It's all right," said the doctor. "It's not broken. Just a sprain. And Grace is going to be fine."

"What on earth were you doing?" asked Ma on the way home.

"We were launching into space," said Grace. "Only our spaceship fell over."

"It was fantastic," Aimee added happily. Her wrist was throbbing but she didn't mind.

"It's a well-known fact that space travel is dangerous," Ma told them. "So I'm going to say right now—and I think Aimee's mom will agree with me—that there are to be no more astronaut games."

"Absolutely," agreed Aimee's mom. "These space explorers are grounded."

"That's okay," said Grace. "We don't want to play astronauts anymore. I want to be a doctor now!"

Calling Doctor Grace

As soon as Nana got back from Texas, she heard about the astronaut adventure. Then Grace said, "Nana, you're not looking at all well. I think you should see the doctor."

"I'm fine, Grace," said Nana, "just a bit tired from the flight."

"I don't think she means just any old doctor," said Ma.

"Oh, I see," said Nana. "You mean Doctor Grace? I'm always glad to see her."

Playing doctor was one of Grace's favorite games. On her last birthday, Ma had given her a costume with a white coat and a wonderful doctor's bag full of instruments and bandages. (Ma secretly hoped that Grace might really be a doctor when she grew up.)

So Nana had to lie down on the sofa and have her temperature taken. "Hmm," said Grace, holding Nana's wrist. "A bad case of anti-rhino. You must take these pills."

"Fine," said Nana. "Would it be all right to take them with a cup of tea?"

"Yes," Grace said, "but only after I've bandaged your leg."

"I didn't know anti-rhino affected the legs," said Ma. "I'd better put the kettle on."

"Oh, yes," Grace told her. "It does when it's a bad case. It starts in the head, but it goes to the legs if you don't get the pills in time."

Soon Nana had a fine bandage on her leg. And since she really was feeling very tired, she didn't mind sitting still and taking her medicine.

"How about you?" Grace asked Ma. "I could check up on your heart."

"You checked it only yesterday," said Ma. "But you can do it again, as long as I can sit down and talk to Nana about her vacation."

That was fine with Grace. She was the kind of doctor who only needed her patients to keep still. So she listened to Ma's heart with her stethoscope and tested her blood pressure and wrote up her notes on the case.

Patient's name: Ma
Illness: Heart sounds broken
Treatment: Bandages

Grace took another of her long bandages and started to wind it around Ma's chest.

"What's this?" asked Ma, reading Grace's notes. "My heart's not broken."

"Patients aren't allowed to know what's wrong with them," said Grace. "It spoils the treatment."

"But surely I should know whether my heart's broken or not," Ma protested. "I mean, it wouldn't work, would it?"

"It'll work if you let me bandage it," said Grace firmly, but she noticed that Ma and Nana exchanged funny looks when they thought she couldn't see.

Grace soon ran out of bandages, so she went off to see if Paw-Paw needed an injection. She was the kind of doctor who didn't mind treating animals.

The game got even better when her friends came over, because Aimee still had her arm in a real sling. Grace set up a hospital in the backyard, putting her patients on deck chairs. To make things look more realistic, Grace got her face paints and Kester painted big red cuts and purple bruises on Raj and Maria. Ma had quite a shock when she came out with lemonade and cookies.

"Gracious! That looks bad, Raj. How did it happen?" she asked.

"I was bitten by a tiger," said Raj proudly.

"And I fell off a mountain," Maria piped up.

"You're lucky you only got a bruise," said Ma. "You might have broken something."

"She did," said Grace. "She broke everything. It's a good thing you brought those bandages back. And I'll need some splints too."

By the end of the day, everyone had a sling or a bandage or a splint. Even Grace, who let Maria borrow her doctor's outfit to treat her, had a big bandage on her foot and was walking with a stick. Of course, everyone had to take off their first-aid dressings before they went home, and Ma insisted that they wash off the face paint, so that their moms wouldn't be frightened.

Grace rolled up her bandages and repacked her bag while Ma and Nana made the dinner. Then she noticed that Ma looked different. She was wearing a new dress and had put on some lipstick.

"Are you going out, Ma?" she asked.

"Yes, honey. I'm going to see a movie with a friend. Nana will be here to look after you."

"That will be fun, won't it, Grace?" said Nana. "We can have a nice long talk. And your poor ma hasn't been out for all the time I've been away."

"Yes, she has," said Grace. "She went to a Chinese restaurant with me. And she went to work every day."

For some reason, Grace felt a bit grumpy about Ma going out on Nana's first night back. And she felt even grumpier when the doorbell rang and she saw that Ma's friend was a man.

"Grace," said Ma, "I want you to meet my friend Vincent. Vince, this is Grace. And you know my mother."

"How do you do?" said Vincent. "Good to meet you, Grace. I see you take after your ma."

Grace let him shake her hand, but she already didn't like him.

When they had gone, Nana said, "Why don't you give me a complete checkup, Grace? That anti-rhino seems to be coming back."

Grace gave Nana a very thorough checkup and lots of medicine. It was only colored water and Nana was very good about taking it. In fact, she was a very good patient altogether, but Grace wasn't happy. She couldn't forget the way Vincent had put his hand under Ma's elbow as they went out the door.

"What's the matter, Doctor?" asked Nana. "Am I a hopeless case?"

"No," said Grace. "But I don't want Ma to marry Vincent."

"Goodness, child," said Nana. "What put that into your head? She has only known him a short while."

"But he seems to like her," said Grace.

"Yes, he does. And that's nice for your ma. She works very hard and she needs a little bit of fun sometimes. It's good for her to have a man friend she can go out with. It doesn't mean they're going to get married."

"Promise?" asked Grace.

"Of course not," said Nana. "Your ma could get married again if she wanted to—she's still young enough."

Grace thought about this. "Is Vincent a doctor?" she asked.

Nana laughed. "No, but he does work at the hospital. He's in the same office as your ma. Would you think it was okay for him to marry her if he was a doctor?"

"No," said Grace. "I don't want her to marry anyone. She has me, doesn't she? And you. Why would she want a husband?"

"I'm not saying she does, Grace," said Nana. "But remember your papa got married again, and you didn't like Jatou at first."

This was too big a thought for Grace. It seemed as if her world was turning upside down.

"Well," said Nana. "I think I'm going to have an early night. All that medicine has made me sleepy. And it's past your bedtime too, Grace."

But as Nana got up off the sofa, Paw-Paw tangled himself in her feet and tripped her. Nana fell to the floor with a crash.

Grace flew to her side. "Nana, Nana, are you all right?"

Nana just groaned.

"Oh, if only I was really a doctor," wailed Grace. But she knew what to do. With trembling fingers she dialed 911 and asked for an ambulance. She told them her name and address and said that her nana had fallen over and hurt herself.

Then she went back to Nana and put a blanket over her to keep her warm. It seemed like ages, but the ambulance actually got there quickly. It didn't have its siren on, but Grace saw the red flashing light through the living-room window.

"She's going to be fine," said the paramedic after checking Nana out. "But we'll have to get her to the hospital. Is your mother here?"

"No, she's gone to the movies," said Grace. "But I don't know which one."

"Then you come along with us and your grandmother. We'll leave your mother a note telling her what's happened. And when she comes to the hospital, we'll tell her what a sensible girl you are."

By now Nana was feeling better, and she told the paramedics, "Of course Grace knew what to do. She's a doctor. Can't you see her white coat?"

Grace sat beside Nana in the back of the ambulance and this time the siren screamed through the night as it raced to the hospital.

The doctor let Grace stay while she examined Nana and arranged for an X ray. When the film came back, the doctor showed Grace the break in Nana's ankle bone.

"You see that, Doctor?" she asked. "That's the end of the tibia."

"Yes, Doctor," said Grace. "Will she have to have a bandage?"

"Oh, yes," said the hospital doctor. "A big bandage, with plaster on top. And she'll have to walk on crutches for a few weeks."

"Oh, poor Nana!" said Grace.

"But she'll be absolutely fine. She's quite lucky. At her age she might have broken her hip, and that's a lot more serious," said the doctor.

Just then, Ma's face appeared around the cubicle curtains.

"What on earth has happened?" she asked. The doctor explained.

"Thanks to your daughter, everything's going to be fine."

Ma gave Grace a hug. "She's a good doctor, isn't she?"

"Yes, she can have a job here any time," said the doctor.

But Grace had a funny feeling that she wouldn't want to play doctor again for a long while.

Grace the Detective

Nana's accident changed everything. There was no way she could cope with having Grace's friends around every day. In fact, Ma had to rearrange her plans and take her vacation a week early (which wasn't an easy thing to do in a busy hospital office) so that she could look after Nana.

Nana hated all the fuss. "It's only a broken ankle," she said. "I've still got all my wits about me and I can still cook."

But once she was back home, even she had to admit that it was awkward and painful getting around on her crutches. And it was too difficult for her to go shopping or use the vacuum cleaner.

For the first few days, she didn't try cooking

either—so it was back to pizza and frozen meals. Grace had a lot to do running around fetching things for Nana—like her glasses, or her book, or her knitting, or the phone.

"You're a great nurse as well as a doctor," said Nana.

But Grace wasn't thinking about hospitals anymore. There was something else on her mind.

Ever since Nana's fall and Ma taking time off work, they had been seeing more and more of Ma's friend Vincent. He came over to take Ma shopping in his car, or he said he was "in the neighborhood" and had stopped by to see how Nana was. He was always taking up space in their living room, always sitting in Grace's usual place on the sofa, often a fourth person at dinner, who was served before Grace.

"I hate it," Grace told Aimee when she went to play at her house.

"Don't you mean *him?*" asked Aimee.

Grace thought about it. "No, I don't think I hate Vincent. He's okay. He's always polite to me and he's really nice to Nana. And I can see he really likes Ma. But we don't need him, and he's always there. He's so *big*."

Aimee laughed. "Well, he can't help that. My dad's big and I don't mind."

"But he's not my dad!" Grace said sharply. Aimee had reminded her of her worst worry. What if Ma and Vince got married? Then he'd always be there. Would she be expected to call him Dad? Grace already had her own papa, who lived in Africa, and she wasn't about to let anyone take his place.

She told Aimee all this.

"Perhaps you'd better ask your ma," suggested Aimee.

"No," said Grace. "She wouldn't tell me. Besides, he might not have asked her yet. I'll have to find out some other way."

Then she had a brilliant idea.

"I know! I'll spy on them! I'll keep a special notebook and write down all the times he comes over and the things he says, and then I'll ask Ma. I'll have real evidence then."

"Wouldn't it be better to spy on just him," asked Aimee, "like a private eye? You might find out he has a wife and ten children."

Grace cheered up. "That would be great!" But

then her face fell. "I couldn't do it. I'm not allowed out on my own."

Still, she liked the private eye idea. Detective was one of her favorite games for playing on her own. Grace went to get her outfit together. She had a battered brown trilby hat of Grandpa's, which she pulled down over her eyes, and an old raincoat of Ma's, which she belted tightly around her middle. She got a notebook and pencil and started watching Ma and Vincent.

MONDAY – Vince to dinner
TUESDAY – Vince dropped in for coffee
WEDNESDAY – Vince took Ma shopping
THURSDAY – Vince took Ma to the movies
FRIDAY –

Well, today was Friday—but Grace could see the pattern already. When Vincent came over that evening to watch a nature program on TV, he found Grace staring at him and writing notes in her book.

The gang got together as usual on Saturday at Grace's. They had fallen into the habit of working next door in Mrs. Myerson's backyard on

Saturday mornings. The little lawn was green now and there were a lot of brightly colored flowers in the beds.

When the kids had finished working, they sprawled on the grass eating homemade gingerbread while Grace told them about Vincent.

"My mom has a boyfriend," said Maria.

"I didn't say he was my mom's boyfriend," said Grace.

"Sounds like it to me," said Kester.

"You can't be sure," Raj told him, waving his cookie. "Remember how you once said Mrs. Myerson would feed us pastries and eat us?"

"Anyway, I don't see what's wrong with it," said Kester. "I wish my mom had a boyfriend. She's been miserable since my dad left."

"But wouldn't you hate having someone taking your dad's place?" asked Grace.

Kester shrugged. "Not really. I'm glad he's not there anymore."

Grace's eyes filled with tears. She couldn't imagine feeling the way Kester did. But she blinked back her tears.

That evening, Vincent was going to take Ma out to dinner. Ma made some pasta and sauce for Nana and Grace before she left. It was good, but after Ma left, Nana said to Grace, "Why don't we make some fudge?"

"Are you sure, Nana? Can you manage?"

"Of course! There's not much cooking in fudge, and you can do most of the work."

Soon they were eating crumbly chocolate fudge with hazelnut chunks. They watched a silly comedy on TV and then Grace washed the dishes and helped Nana get ready for bed.

"It's as if I'm baby-sitting you, instead of the other way around," she said.

"Not so much of the baby," said Nana. "You're granny-sitting, that's all, and a fine job you're doing. Now fetch me my paper, and you'd better be getting ready for bed yourself."

But Grace had other plans. She put on her detective hat and coat and took her notebook, and sat by the living-room window in the dark, watching out for Ma and Vincent. But a private eye who is full of pasta and fudge finds it hard to stay awake, and she soon nodded off.

The sound of a car door slamming woke her up. She heard two people talking and laughing outside the front door. Grace had her nose pressed hard against the window.

Then Ma's key turned in the door and Grace heard her inviting Vincent in for hot chocolate. Oh no, thought Grace. They'll come in here and find me.

She curled herself up small on the window-sill and hid as quietly as she could behind the curtain. The lights snapped on. Ma and Vince walked through the living room into the kitchen. Grace heard the mugs clattering and then the sound of a kettle boiling, while Ma and Vincent talked in low voices.

Then she heard them coming back into the living room. Ma turned on the radio and music began to play softly. The curtain moved, and Grace nearly screamed. It was Paw-Paw, wanting to see who was hiding on the windowsill. He was delighted to find Grace behind the curtain, and started purring loudly. Then he tried to climb on her lap, which wasn't really there because Grace's knees were nearly touching her chest.

But Paw-Paw was a determined cat and he forced his way onto where her lap should have

been. One of Grace's legs slipped off the windowsill and Paw-Paw started to knead her lap. His claws were sharp and Grace couldn't help herself.

"Ow!" she cried, and fell from her hiding place onto the floor with a thud.

Vincent was so startled, he spilled his hot chocolate on the sofa. There was a flurry of activity while Ma got a towel to clean it up, and Vincent kept apologizing.

"Don't worry," said Ma grimly. "It wasn't your fault. It's Grace who ought to be saying sorry. What on earth do you think you're doing, Grace?"

"It's late," said Vincent. "I think I'd better be going."

When he had gone, Ma came and sat Grace down next to her on the sofa.

"Now, what was all that about?" she said. "As if I don't know. Look at you! All dressed up like a detective. You've been spying on me."

Grace hung her head. It was true. "I'm sorry, Ma," she said. "I didn't mean to embarrass you. I was just keeping an eye on Vincent."

"Why? What has he done?"

"Well, he has been around here a lot."

"That's not a crime, is it?" Ma asked.

"No."

"Well, detectives are usually on the track of crimes, aren't they? What do you think is wrong with Vince being here?"

"I don't want you to get married!" Grace said loudly.

"Get married! Whatever gave you that idea?"

"I saw him kiss you," said Grace, and she burst into tears.

Ma took Grace into her arms and cuddled her until she stopped crying.

"You see what trouble your games can get you into?" she said. "Vince and I aren't getting married. I've only known him a few months. But we are going out together."

"So is he your boyfriend?" asked Grace.

"Yes, I guess you could say he is," said Ma, laughing. "Though that makes us sound like teenagers. Don't you like him?"

"He's okay," said Grace. "I just don't see why you need him when you've got Nana and me."

"Well, why do you need Aimee? And Raj and Maria and Kester? You've got Nana and me, but you still have to have other people in your life, don't you?"

"Ye-es," Grace said slowly. "Are you sure you're not going to marry him?"

"No, honey, I'm not absolutely certain. But it's too soon to think about that."

"Do you like him more than Papa?" asked Grace.

Ma sighed. "That's a really hard question. I like him a lot and that's all I'm thinking about at the moment."

Grace snuggled up close to Ma's silky dress. "You smell nice," she said.

"So do you," said Ma. "In fact, you smell of fudge."

"That's because we made some," said Grace, springing up off the sofa. "And there's a lot left in the fridge. Would you like a little?"

"There's only one thing I'd like more," said Ma. "And that's for you to take off that hat and coat and think of a new game!"

So Grace stopped being a detective and instead dipped pieces of fudge in Ma's hot chocolate. And she went to bed happier than she had been for a long time.

Grace and the Time Machine

Nana was a lot better, so the gang was allowed to come back and play at Grace's place. Ma returned to work and things were more or less back to normal.

But Nana's leg was still in a cast, and even though she could get around very quickly on her crutches, she found it difficult to bend down or reach up.

Grace and the others were always picking things up for her, or climbing onto chairs to get things down from high places.

"It's lovely to have so many extra arms and legs," said Nana gratefully.

"But what about when we're not here?" said Grace. "We should invent something to help you pick up things."

"Yes," said Raj. "Let's be inventors. We can invent all sorts of things."

"Maybe we'll get rich," said Maria.

The next hour was a very messy one in Grace's kitchen. Every utensil was tipped out of the kitchen drawers and a lot of string and packing tape was used. Eventually the inventors proudly presented Nana with a pair of tongs with salad servers and wooden spoons attached to them.

The children made Nana drop her glasses on the rug and then showed her how to pick them up with the tongs, without bending down.

"If that doesn't beat everything!" said Nana. "Thank you. It's a wonderful invention."

But when Ma came home and they started making dinner, they found it diffult to manage without all the pieces of the picking-up machine. They had to toss the salad with a spoon and fork, which was all right, and turn the sausages with two more forks, which was awkward, and it was hard for Nana to make gravy without a wooden spoon.

"It was very kind of you to invent this gadget for Nana," said Ma after they had eaten. "But you know, I think someone has already invented it and I can get it from the hospital."

The next day Grace's face fell when she saw the gray metal grabber. It was much better than the tong contraption.

"So we didn't invent anything after all," she said.

"But you thought of it, Grace," said Ma. "And I didn't. I could have gotten one of these for Nana weeks ago."

Grace was cheered up a bit. But the others were very disapppointed.

"All that time," said Aimee, "and we just invented something that already existed."

"We have to think of something that no one else has thought of," said Raj. "That's what real inventors do."

"Oh, is that all?" said Kester. "It should be easy, then."

"Don't squabble," said Grace. "We must all think hard of something we wish existed, but doesn't. Something that would be useful to us."

"Grass that doesn't need cutting," said Maria, who was fed up with the blunt shears they had to use on Mrs. Myerson's lawn every Saturday.

"Skateboards with brakes," said Kester, who had a big blue bruise on his knee.

"That's what feet are for," Raj told him. "I'd like a machine that would read books for you."

How horrible! thought Grace, but she didn't say anything, because she knew Raj found reading very hard.

"I think," said Aimee, "I'd like something that would make you taller, but not hurt."

Aimee was very self-conscious about being short, and didn't believe her mother when she told her she would soon shoot up.

"What about you, Grace?" asked Maria.

"I'd like to invent a time machine," said Grace.

"Hey, that's cheating," Kester protested. "You said to think of something useful!"

"It *would* be useful," said Maria. "You could go forward in time and find out the questions for a math test."

"Or go back and change things," suggested Kester.

"Yes, you could go back and pick Paw-Paw up, so that he didn't trip Nana," said Aimee.

They agreed that the time machine would be

the best invention of all. And since the other things would be just as difficult to invent without being scientists and having laboratories, they decided to concentrate on the time machine.

"Dials," said Raj. "You have to have dials and clocks and things."

"And wheels," said Grace.

"And maybe wings," said Maria.

Grace's backyard was soon so full of odds and ends, it looked like a junkyard. There was an old radio that didn't work anymore, two alarm clocks, Nana's kitchen timer, Grace's bicycle, five kitchen chairs, and a big beach umbrella.

This time there was room for all five children in the contraption they built and it really did look like a mad inventor's time-traveling machine. They had a wonderful afternoon traveling around the world. (Grace's atlas was propped up on the bicycle handlebars, so that they could choose places as well as times.)

Kester chose to go into the future with Raj while Grace, Maria, and Aimee walked around with saucepans on their heads pretending to be future people.

Maria and Aimee went back to the dinosaur ages and Raj was a Tyrannosaurus, while Grace was a Triceratops and Kester a Stegosaur. There was so much roaring that Nana hobbled to the back door to see what was the matter. She shook her head when she saw the time machine.

Grace wanted to go to Africa with Aimee and Kester. "That's not time travel," objected Raj.

"All right then," said Grace. "Make it last year when I went to The Gambia."

Aimee ran to fetch the crocodile again and Raj played the drums, while Maria danced what she thought might be an African dance.

"How lovely!" said Grace, stepping out of the time machine. "It is so hot here in Africa."

"Have some mango," said Maria. "And what else do you get in Africa?"

"Melon," said Grace, "and papaya and passion fruit and jackfruit."

"Well, let's have those things too," said Maria.

"Let's give Nana a turn," said Aimee. "She could get into the time machine without any trouble."

So they went to fetch Nana and she carefully

sat in one of the chairs, balancing her crutches against the bicycle.

"Choose a place," said Kester, showing her the atlas.

"No question," said Nana. "Trinidad, where I was born."

She found it on the map and showed it to them.

"And when would you like it to be?" asked Maria.

"Oh," said Nana, "when I was a little girl about your age. Let's say sixty years ago."

Maria adjusted the radio dial, set the two alarm clocks, and made the kitchen timer ring.

"Let me help you out of the machine," said Grace. "You are now in Trinidad."

Nana was very used to playing Grace's games. She got out of the time machine and looked around her full of wonder, just like a little girl, even though she still had crutches.

"Oh, how wonderful!" she said in a little girl's voice, pointing at the house with her crutches. "There's the house where I grew up. See the purple bougainvillea growing up the side of it? And over there is the path down to the beach where the fishermen catch crabs in their pots. I bet my brother Maxie is down there playing in the sand. And listen! I can hear my mother calling me . . . Lucie . . . Lucie!"

The children listened. Nana made it all seem so real. Then they did hear the voice. "Lucie . . . Lucie."

"The time machine!" gasped Grace. "It worked!"

Then they saw Mrs. Myerson looking over the fence. She was calling Nana.

"Whatever is that?" she said, looking at the time machine.

"Hello, Gerda," said Nana in her ordinary voice. "It's a wonderful machine that can take you back to when you were small."

"Or into the future," said Kester. "If you prefer."

"Would you like a turn, Mrs. Myerson?" asked Raj.

"We could come and walk you around," offered Grace, who knew that the woman was scared of going out in the street. They all thought that she would say no, but Mrs. Myerson did come and try the time machine.

She chose Germany as the place and 1925 as

the year. Old Mrs. Myerson looked very strange, sitting upright in one of Grace's kitchen chairs, closing her eyes and muttering while Raj set the dials.

Then, when she opened her bright dark eyes, it was as if she couldn't see the children in the backyard at all.

"Heidelberg," she whispered. "My grandparents' house with the big backyard. They are all here, Mutti and Papa, my cousin Franz, my sister Hilde, my other cousins Fritz and Lili, oh, and the dogs . . . so many dogs. It is a summer day and we are playing in the brook at the bottom of the backyard. Fritz is catching minnows and splashing my dress. Oh, and it's such a pretty dress—white with a blue sash."

The children held their breath. Mrs. Myerson had never told them anything about her family before. Now they were coming alive before their eyes.

"Hilde is picking flowers for the dinner table," Mrs. Myerson went on. "Lilies and roses. Franz asks her for a rose for his buttonhole and she gives him a pink one with a heavenly scent. I can smell it now."

Suddenly she stopped, and the children saw she was crying. They felt terrible. But she wiped her eyes with a lacy handkerchief and said, "Thank you, children. It is a wonderful machine."

"I think it's time to come back to the present and have a good strong cup of tea," said Nana.

But Mrs. Myerson insisted on finishing the game properly. She climbed back into the machine and had the dials reset before she went into the kitchen with Nana.

"It's a miracle," Nana told Ma that evening. "Not only did Gerda Myerson walk here from her house—she told us all about her childhood. She remembered how happy she was."

"It was just as if she really did travel back in time," said Grace.

"Then your machine works," said Ma. "What a wonderful invention!"

Starring Grace

⸻⸺⸻

The next mail delivery brought Grace a large envelope with a crocodile stamp on it. It was her monthly letter from Africa, and it was satisfyingly fat. There was a letter from Papa, which she saved to read later, two chatty pages from Jatou, a note from Neneh, and a picture from Bakary. It was a crayon drawing of an animal, which could have been anything, but Neneh had written "Corned Beef" underneath, which was the name of their dog.

Grace pinned the picture to her bulletin board and put the letters from Jatou and Neneh in her stationery folder. Then she took Papa's letter out to the backyard to read in her special place under the tree. It reminded her of the jackfruit tree in the backyard of Papa's compound in The Gambia, where she used to sit with him in the warm evenings when her little brother and sister had gone to bed.

The letter was a lovely one, full of details about the family's life. Grace closed her eyes after she had read it and, with the sun on her face, imagined herself back in Bakau. She could almost smell the ocean.

A shadow fell across her face, blocking out the sun.

"A penny for your thoughts, Grace," said Nana.

"I was wishing my time machine really worked," said Grace. "I went back to Africa in it, but it was only playing. I'm still here and Papa is *miles* away."

"You know what?" said Nana, settling down in her deck chair. "I think we all have a kind of time machine in our heads. When I came out, I swear *you* were miles away. I bet you were in Africa with your papa."

"Yes, I was," said Grace, surprised. Then she looked sad again. "But it was only pretend."

"Pretending is making up things that haven't happened," Nana explained. "What you were doing was remembering something that *did* happen. That's quite different. But pretending is good too, and you are very good at it. Just think of all the pretending you have done this summer with your friends."

"Yes," said Grace. "We pretended a ghost and found Mrs. Myerson. And we pretended a jungle and found a backyard."

"I wonder whether you'd all like to do some more pretending," said Nana.

"What do you mean?" asked Grace.

"Well, my paper says the local theater is putting on a musical and they're looking for some kids to be extras."

"A real show? In a real theater?"

After that, there was no holding Grace back. As soon as her friends came over, she showed them the advertisement in the paper. Kester and Aimee both wanted to go to the audition, but Maria and Raj weren't so sure.

"I'd rather watch," said Maria.

"I'd like to help with the lights," said Raj.

"Oh, come on," said Grace. "It'll only be fun if we all do it."

So in the end they all did. They turned up

at the theater on Saturday afternoon and waited in line with a lot of other children of many different ages and sizes. The musical was "Annie" and the girl who was going to be Annie had already been chosen. She was much older than Grace and her friends—in fact, she was fifteen—but she was small for her age and had been acting for years. Her name was Brianna and she was really friendly. She put on a curly red wig to show them.

"I'll have freckles too," she said, "when the makeup people have finished with me."

Grace was in seventh heaven. She loved the smell of the theater, which had red plush tip-up seats like the ones in the theater where Nana had once taken her to see the ballet.

A busy lady with a clipboard took their names.

"Orphans on this side, street urchins over there," she said.

"I don't know if I'm an orphan or an urchin," whispered Kester.

"The orphans all have to be girls," said Grace, who knew "Annie" by heart. "You'll have to be a street urchin."

"Then I'll be one too," said Raj.

So the two boys went over to the other side and Maria went with them.

"If I have to be in the play, I'm not going to be an orphan," she said. "Street urchins sound like more fun."

Grace and Aimee liked the idea of being orphans, because they got to sing. First they watched all the boys and some girls being led across the stage, while the clipboard lady whispered to a bearded man sitting in a tip-up seat right in the middle of the theater.

"He must be the director," whispered Grace.

Only about a quarter of the boys and girls were asked to stay. Kester, Maria, and Raj were all chosen. A lot of girls wanted to be Annie's orphan friends, and they had to go up in batches while they were taught the tune and words to "It's the Hard-Knock Life." A lady with frizzy ginger hair and a big bosom played a piano at the side of the stage.

"I'm getting very tired of that song," said Ma to Nana.

"We knew it pretty well already, didn't we, Ava?" said Nana, winking at Grace.

But Grace wasn't tired of any of it. When it was her turn to go up on the stage with the other girls, she felt so excited, she started to dance, even though they hadn't been taught any steps. She knew the words without looking at the blackboard. It was one of her favorite songs.

The clipboard lady called Grace and Aimee over, and they were chosen too! Afterward the gang went back to Grace's house and talked excitedly in the backyard. Maria and Raj had forgotten about not wanting to be in the play.

"It was so cool," said Maria, "being on stage in a real theater. Much better than the school auditorium."

"And we get to wear rags!" said Kester with a big grin.

"We don't have any words to learn, though," said Aimee, "apart from the songs."

"Good," said Raj. "It wouldn't be fun if we had to learn speeches."

But Grace wouldn't have minded learning speeches. She had a private dream that Brianna might get sick and then she, Grace, would step in to play her part, red wig and all. She *did* know all the words.

Grace and Aimee didn't have named parts; none of the local children did. All the orphans who had things to say, like Molly, Pepper, and July, were played by older girls like Brianna. But Grace and her friends had to go to just as many rehearsals as the main actors. Nana took them and picked them up every day. Her ankle was better now.

"This show has come along at the right time," she told Grace. "You were all beginning to be bored with nothing to do but play."

It was true. The gang had thought of just about everything they could play that summer, and there were still two weeks before they went back to school. "Annie" was going to start in six weeks' time.

"All the kids who went to camp are going to be so jealous," said Maria. "They didn't even get the chance to audition."

The days flew by. The orphans had song and dance routines to master, which they practiced over and over again. And the street urchins had to learn movements that were just as compli-cated as dance steps. There were a lot of them and they had to be in their right places on stage at all times.

It was very tiring, but they had many breaks and drinks and chocolate cookies. The actor playing Daddy Warbucks was a nice, funny man named Eric. He had a great deal of brown hair, but he was going to wear a bald "wig" for the performances. And there was going to be a real dog playing Sandy. He was specially trained, but he didn't come to the early rehearsals. Grace couldn't wait to see him; she loved dogs.

The children went back to school in the first week of September. Natalie had been to France and some of the children had traveled even farther. But no one was in the musical except for Grace and her friends.

"We should call ourselves the Annie Gang now," said Aimee.

The only thing Grace was sad about was that Papa would not be able to see her acting in a real play. She wrote him a long letter describing it. And Ma promised to take photos and have two sets developed so that Grace could send one set to Papa.

Brianna stayed healthy. But on the day of the dress rehearsal, Lara, the girl playing July, came down with a bad case of laryngitis. She couldn't speak at all! Daniel Laski, the bearded director, sent his assistant, Emma, the clipboard lady, to the crowded dressing room. It was full of "orphans" having dirt smudges carefully applied to their faces, and their clean shiny hair mussed up with gray powder.

"Grace, can you come and speak to Daniel?" asked Emma. Grace's heart started to pound. Perhaps he wanted her to be Annie after all! But he just asked if she knew the words July had to say.

"I've watched you during rehearsals," he said. "And I think you know all the parts."

Grace couldn't speak, but she nodded.

"Could you step in for Lara, just until she gets her voice back?" he asked. "You'd be doing us a big favor. Of course, you are very young to have a speaking part, so I'll quite understand if your parents don't want you to do it. We have to have their permission."

"I'll get my nana now," said Grace and rushed off to find her.

But Nana wouldn't say yes right away.

"You know I'll have to ask your ma, Grace," she said.

Mr. Laski said they could use the phone in his office. "I really need to get this sorted out as soon as possible," he said.

Nana rang Ma at the hospital. Grace anxiously watched Nana's face as she explained everything. "Mm hm. . . . Uh-huh. . . . Right. . . . Okay, I understand. . . . Yes, I'll tell him." Then Nana put the phone down. Grace was sure that Ma had said no.

"She says yes," said Nana, and Grace gave a big squeal and danced Nana all around Mr. Laski's office. He was laughing and trying to get out of their way.

"Here's the form for Grace's mother to sign," he said. "Bring it to the theater tomorrow."

The next day was the big one. First night. The theater was sold out. Grace peeped through a gap in the curtain and saw Ma and Nana sitting a few rows back. And there was Vincent, sitting beside Ma. I might have known, she thought. But then she thought, I'm glad he's here. I want everyone to see me.

Then she noticed someone else, next to Nana. It was Mrs. Myerson! But there was no time to wonder about that; the orchestra players were coming into the pit and Emma shooed the children away from the curtain back to the dressing rooms.

Grace wasn't in the big dressing room with all the other orphans now. She was sharing a smaller one with the girls playing Molly and Duffy and Pepper. Brianna was in there too, putting on her wig. There was a knock at the door. It was Aimee.

"I came to say good luck, Grace," she said.

"Thank you," said Grace. She suddenly felt shy.

"What we say in the theater is 'break a leg,'" said Brianna, laughing.

"I wouldn't dare say that anywhere near Grace," said Aimee.

Then it was time to go on. Grace had the time of her life. It was as good as being Peter Pan—better, in some ways. Although she wasn't the main character, she was in a real theater, with real footlights and spotlights, and a real red velvet curtain with gold braid and tassels.

When the show was over and the cast had taken four curtain calls, Ma and Nana and Vincent and Mrs. Myerson came backstage to find

Grace, and they all had flowers for her. Grace's arms were full of bouquets.

Then Ma gave her an extra one: "These came for you this afternoon." It was a bouquet of roses and the card said:

> For Grace, the famous actor, from her loving papa and her African family.

Grace buried her face in all her flowers.

"It was only a small part," she said.

"Honey," said Ma, "as far as we are concerned, you were the star of the show."

"Yes," said Nana. "Whatever she does, Grace is always a star."

Mary Hoffman has written more than seventy books for children, including the best-selling *Amazing Grace*. *Publishers Weekly* hailed it as "truly inspiring." Its sequel, *Boundless Grace*, was praised by *School Library Journal* for being a "universal story that is uplifting and bound to please." Ms. Hoffman and her husband have three daughters and they live in England.

Caroline Binch is the multiple-award-winning illustrator of *Amazing Grace* and *Boundless Grace*. One of the most popular books of 1991, *Amazing Grace* appeared on the *Publishers Weekly* best-seller list for six months. Ms. Binch also illustrated *Hue Boy*, a *New York Times* Best Illustrated Book, and wrote and illustrated *Gregory Cool*, which was shortlisted for the Kate Greenaway Medal. Ms. Binch lives in England.